THE FAMOUS FIVE

SHORT STORIES

FIVE
HAVE A
PUZZLING
TIME

The Famous Five

Timmy   Anne   Dick   Julian   George

Text copyright © Hodder & Stoughton Ltd, 1956
Illustrations copyright © Hodder & Stoughton Ltd, 2014

Enid Blyton's signature is a registered trademark of Hodder & Stoughton Ltd

This is an abridgement of the text first published
in Great Britain in *Enid Blyton's Magazine Annual – No. 3*, in 1956.
First published in Great Britain in this edition in 2014 by Hodder Children's Books.

The rights of Enid Blyton and Jamie Littler to be identified as the Author
and Illustrator of the Work respectively have been asserted by them in
accordance with the Copyright, Designs and Patents Act 1988

1

A Catalogue record for this book is available from the British Library
ISBN 978 1 444 916317

Hodder Children's Books
A division of Hachette Children's Books
Hachette UK Limited, 338 Euston Road, London NW1 3BH

www.hachette.co.uk

Enid Blyton

FIVE HAVE A PUZZLING TIME

illustrated by **Jamie Littler**

h

*Hodder
Children's
Books*

A division of Hachette Children's Books

Famous Five Colour Reads

For a complete list of the full-length
Famous Five adventures, turn to
the last page of this book

Contents

CHAPTER ONE

It was dark and very quiet in Kirrin Cottage –
almost midnight.

'**Poor George,**' said Anne. 'Good thing
you're going to the **dentist tomorrow!**'

'**Don't remind me of that!**' said
George, walking up and down the bedroom.
'Go to sleep, Anne – I didn't mean to
disturb you.'

George went to the window and **looked out** over **Kirrin Bay.** Timmy jumped off the bed and stood beside her, paws on the windowsill. Suddenly George stiffened and frowned. She stared across the bay, and then turned and called urgently to Anne.

'**Anne! Quick, wake up! Come and see!** There's a **light** shining out on **Kirrin Island! Somebody's there – on *MY* island!**'

Anne sat up sleepily. 'What's the matter, George? What did you say?'

'I said, there's **a light on Kirrin Island! Somebody** must be there – **without permission too!** I'll get **my boat** and **row out right now!**'

George was **very angry** indeed, and Timmy gave a little **growl.** He would most certainly deal with whoever it was on the island!

George went quickly down to where Dick and Julian lay asleep and shook them roughly. **'Wake up!** Something's going on over at Kirrin Island. **WAKE UP, Julian.'**

George's excited voice not only woke up the boys, but her father as well. Everybody met in the boys' room. 'What on earth is all this about?' demanded George's father.

'There's a light on Kirrin Island,' said George. 'I'm going to see who it is – and so is Timmy. If no one will come with me I'll go alone.'

'Indeed you won't go,' said her father, raising his voice angrily. **'Get back to bed!** You can go over **tomorrow.'**

'I can't!' almost wailed George. 'I've got to go to the dentist. **I must go tonight!'**

'Shut up, George,' said Julian. 'Be sensible. Whoever's there will still be there tomorrow. Anyway, there's no light there now – you probably made a mistake.'

CHAPTER TWO.

'Poor George,' said Anne, as the car went off down the road. 'She does get so worked up about things.'

'Well, anyone gets upset with toothache,' said Julian.

He stared out over Kirrin Bay, which was as blue as cornflowers that morning. 'I wonder if George *did* see a light on the island last night? You didn't see one, did you, Anne?'

'No. It was all dark there,' said Anne. 'Honestly, I think George must have **dreamt it!** Anyway she can take out her boat this afternoon, and we'll go with her, and **have a good look round!'**

'I tell you what,' said Dick, 'we **three** will get the **boat** and go over to the **island this morning** – then, when we find nothing and nobody there – except the rabbits and the jackdaws – we can tell George, and she **won't worry any more!'**

'Right!' said Julian. 'Let's go now, **straight away!** Uncle Quentin will be glad to be rid of us – he's working hard this morning on one of his newest problems.'

They went to the beach, to get **George's boat.** There it was, **ready waiting!** Julian looked across to where Kirrin Island lay peacefully in the sun. He was **quite certain** there was **nobody there!**

'We'll row right round the island and see
if there's a boat tied up anywhere, or beached,'
said Dick, taking the oars. 'If there isn't, we'll
know there's no one there. It's too far for
anyone to swim to. Well – **here we go!**'

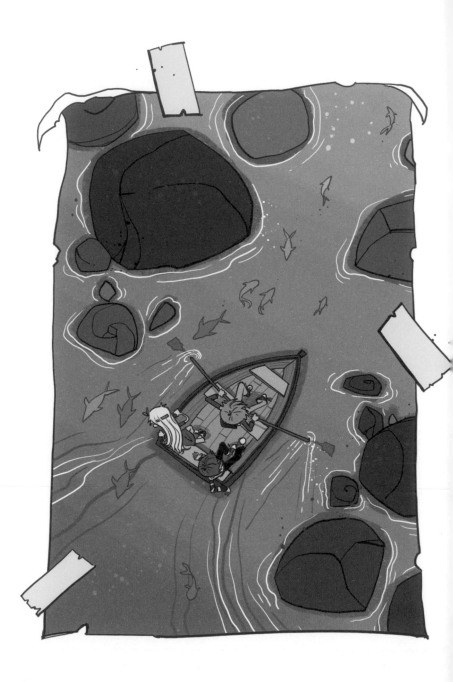

CHAPTER THREE

Dick rowed the boat carefully between the rocks that guarded the island. 'We'll land at our usual little cove,' he said. 'I'll bet no one else would know how to get there if they didn't **already know the way!'**

'The water's like glass here,' said Anne. 'I can see the bottom of the cove.' She leapt out and helped the boys to pull in the boat.

They came to the **old ruined castle** that had been built long ago on the island. Now the jackdaws came down from the tower, and chacked loudly round them in a very friendly manner.

'Well – it doesn't look as if anyone's here,' said Julian, staring round and about.

They went in and out of the old castle, examining the floor – but there was **no sign** of anyone having made a fire. No matter how they searched, the three could find nothing to explain the light that George had said she saw.

Anne sat down and undid her sandals. She set them by a big stone, so that she could **easily find them** again, and ran down to the sea.

Soon Julian and Dick came back together, having gone all round the island, and looked into every cranny. They called to Anne.

'We **haven't** seen a sign of a single soul,' said Dick. 'Better go home again. George may be back by now.'

'I'll put on my sandals,' said Anne, drying her feet in the warm sand. She ran to the big stone by which she had put them. She stopped – and stared in surprise. 'What's happened to one of my sandals? Dick – Ju – have you taken one?'

'Sandals? No – we didn't even know where you'd put them,' said Julian. 'There's **one** of them there, look – the other must be somewhere near.'

But it wasn't.

'**Well! How silly!**' said Anne, amazed. 'I know I put them both together, just here. Anyway, **why take one,** and **not both?**'

'Perhaps a rabbit took one?' suggested Dick, with a grin. 'Or a jackdaw – they're really mischievous birds, you know!'

'A jackdaw surely **couldn't** pick up **a sandal!**' said Anne. 'It'd be too heavy. And I can't imagine a rabbit running off with one!'

'Well – it's not there,' said Dick, thinking that Anne must have been mistaken about putting them both by the big stone. He hunted round, but could not see the other one anywhere – **STRANGE!**

CHAPTER FOUR

They were soon all in the boat again, and the
boys took it in turn to row back. Through the
crowd of rocks they went, threading their way
carefully, and at last came to their own beach.

George was there, waiting for them,
Timmy beside her!

'You went **without me!'** she
scolded. '**You really are horrible!**
What did you find?'

'**Nothing** and **no one.** The island's absolutely **empty** except for rabbits and jackdaws!' said Julian, dragging the boat up the sand.

'How's the tooth, George?' said Anne, seeing that George's cheek was still swollen.

But George didn't want to talk about her tooth. '**It's out,**' she said, shortly. 'If I hadn't had to go to the dentist, I could have gone with you – and I *BET* Timmy and I would have **found** something.'

'All right – go there, then – and take Tim with you,' said Dick, exasperated.

'That's just what I will do!' said George with a scowl. 'We'll soon find out who's hiding there. You can come, too, if you like, of course – but I can't see that you'll be much use!'

'Oh, we'll come all right!' said Dick. 'Even if it's only to say, "Told you so" when **you** can't find more than **we did!**'

George had made up her mind to go off in her boat after she had had her dinner.

It wasn't a very happy meal. Even Joanna the cook added a few cross words as she cleared away. 'I'd like to know who's been at the **grapes** and the **oranges,**' she said. '**Someone** came downstairs in the night and **helped themselves.** And George – what did you do with the bag of **dog biscuits**? I **couldn't find any** for Tim's dinner.'

'Oh don't fuss, Joanna!' said George. 'You know where I always put them – in the outhouse, with the chicken food.'

'Well, you didn't this time,' said Joanna, huffily.

'I'd like to know something now,' said George. **'Who's** been at **my big box** of *chocolates?*' She had opened a large box, and was staring inside. 'There's more than **half gone!'**

But she took herself in hand, helped Joanna with the washing up, and then went to look for the **biscuits** for Timmy. Sure enough, **THEY WERE MISSING,** as Joanna had said.

CHAPTER FIVE

They soon came to the island. George circled it deftly in the boat, being anxious herself to see that no one had hidden another boat anywhere. She pointed to where a great mass of brown **SEAWEED** had piled up on the west shore.

'See what the wind did when we had that **terrific gale** on Tuesday – brought in masses of **SEAWEED** again!

Hey – what's wrong with the **jackdaws,** all of a sudden? Why are they flying up in such a hurry? **There *is* someone on the island!'**

George swung the boat round and ran it deftly into the little cove. Out they all leapt, and pulled in the boat. Timmy tore up the beach at full speed, barking.

'That'll scare the life out of anyone hiding!' said George, pleased. 'Go on, Tim – bark. **Hunt around! Sniff everywhere!'**

They came to a group of bushes and Timmy began to sniff about at once.

'He can smell something there!' said George, excited. **'What is it, Tim?'**

But apparently he found nothing of interest, and soon joined them again. Then Anne's sharp eyes caught sight of something bright under a bush.

'**Look – orange peel!** Someone *must* have **been here then!** We'd never leave orange peel about! And look, what's this!'

They all clustered round and looked where Anne was pointing. George bent down and picked up something very small.

'See – a pip – **a pip from a grape.** Does that ring a bell, anyone?'

'**Yes!**' said Dick. 'Joanna said we'd been at the oranges and grapes – do you think that . . .'

'No! **Who's** going to **steal** a bit of **fruit** and take it over to the island to eat!' said Julian. 'That's too far-fetched, honestly! Let's be sensible!'

'**What's Timmy doing?**' said Anne, suddenly.

Timmy was feverishly scraping at the sand nearby with his front paws. He gave an excited little bark, that sounded pleased. What on earth had he found?

The others ran to him at once.

Timmy had **made a hole** – and in it something showed. Timmy took hold of it with his teeth, and pulled. It split at once – and to everyone's enormous astonishment, out came **a mass of dog biscuits!**

CHAPTER SIX

Surely, surely they couldn't be the **biscuits** that George had bought for Timmy the day before, and put in the outhouse?

'They are!' said George. 'Look – exactly the same kind. Who on earth would want to steal dog biscuits and bring them here – and oranges and grapes – and for goodness' sake, **WHY?'**

'Well, that settles it,' said Julian. **'You were right, George** – someone is here. But how did they get here **without a boat?' 'We'll soon find out!'** said George grimly. 'We know he's **a thief,** anyway! **Tim!** Find him, **find him**, whoever he is! **Smell him out,** Tim!'

Over the sand and on to the rocks went Timmy, right up to where the **SEAWEED** was piled in **great masses** by the wind and the waves. He stopped and began to sniff anxiously.

'He's lost the trail!' said George, disappointed. 'It's the **smell** of the **SEAWEED** that's put him off.'

'Or else whoever was here came in a boat **at high tide,** which would bring it to the shore – and has sailed off again now the tide has gone out,' said Julian, frowning. 'There **wouldn't** be any **trail to smell,** then.'

'Timmy – sniff round again,' said George. 'Go on – you may pick up some other trail.'

Timmy obediently sniffed here and there, and occasionally gave a strange growl of anger. **Why?** George was puzzled.

George wanted to go on hunting, but the others felt that it was no use. If Timmy had found the scent, and **couldn't** follow it, **no one** else would be **able to!** Anyway, probably the trespasser was far away by now, safely in his boat!

They went back to where they had left their 𝒷𝒾𝓈𝒸𝓊𝒾𝓉𝓈 and bars of *chocolate*, Anne stopped suddenly and stared down in amazement. **'Look!** Half the 𝒷𝒾𝓈𝒸𝓊𝒾𝓉𝓈 **have gone** – and two of the *chocolate* **bars!** Surely the jackdaws couldn't have taken them so quickly!'

'There's a **broken** biscuit over here, look – it must have been **dropped!'** said Dick, amazed. **'I didn't hear a thing!'**

'Nor did Tim – or he would have barked,' said George, really puzzled. 'Whoever it was must have come up as **quietly as a mouse!'**

'Let Timmy sniff round – he'll pick up the trail,' said Julian. **'It'll be so fresh!'**

Timmy ran a little way, nose to ground – and then stopped, as if the **trail** had **come to an end!**

'Look, Timmy – trails don't finish all of a sudden!' said George, exasperated. 'People don't take off in mid-air!'

'Well, let's hunt round a bit again,' said Julian. 'I know – we'll **leave** some biscuits and the barley sugars here, **and hide** – and maybe the thief will come along and **take** those. He seems to have a **sweet tooth!'**

'**Good idea,'** said Dick. 'Come on, everyone – you too, Timmy – and **not a sound from anyone,** mind!'

They went behind the gorse bush and waited. Dick peeped out once or twice, but the **bag of** barley sugars remained **untouched.**

Then suddenly Timmy gave a **low** **growl, leapt out** and **ran** **at something!**

Everyone followed in excitement. Who was it? There was **nobody there!**

But up on one of the branches of the nearby **tree** sat **the thief,** a barley sugar clutched in his hand, chattering angrily. **'It's a monkey** – a little **monkey!'** cried George, in the greatest astonishment. 'It was he who **took** the **other things!** Wherever did he come from?'

'Of course!' said Julian. **'This is a puzzle!** What do we do next?'

CHAPTER SEVEN

'Well, there's one thing we do know – and that is that a monkey wouldn't light a fire or a lamp at night on the island,' said Dick. 'That must have been done by a human being – and he **MUST still be on the island** if his monkey's here.'

'Follow the trail again, Tim,' said Julian. 'You may do better this time. **Go on!'**

But before Timmy could put his head down again, something odd happened. A **strange noise** came from the west side of the island – the

MISERABLE

HOWLING of a dog!

'Oh, quick – he sounds as if **he's in trouble!**' cried George. 'What's happening? **Quick, Julian, quick, Timmy!** Oh, poor thing, there he goes, howling again. We must find him,

we must!'

The Five set off in the direction of the howls, Timmy racing ahead anxiously. He knew far better than the others that a dog was in sore trouble – a howling of that kind meant not only **pain,** but **terror.**

Julian was now in front of the other three, and was heading for the **SEAWEED** spread shore on the west of the island. George suddenly gave a cry, and pointed.

'There's the
monkey again!
He's seen us – **he's** **racing away!'**
'Maybe he'll **lead** us to wherever the
dog is,' shouted Julian.

The monkey scampered in front, just
ahead of Timmy. They all came to the shore,
and stopped when they came to the piled-up
heaps of **SEAWEED**.

They watched the tiny brown monkey. He was making his way over the seaweed-covered rocks now, avoiding the pools of water here and there. Further and further out he went. George started to go, too, but Julian pulled her back.

'No. That **SEAWEED** is slippery – it's **too dangerous** to go out on those rocks – we know the sea is very deep in between. Look at that little monkey – where on earth does he think he's going?'

The monkey came to a **rock** that was absolutely **covered** with thick masses of **SEAWEED** flung there by the surging, wind-blown tide. He had no sooner arrived there than **an extraordinary thing happened!**

A small mass of seaweed moved – and out of it came something that made the **Five** stare in utter disbelief.

'It can't be!' muttered Dick. 'No – it can't be!'

It was the brown and white head of a **big dog!** The head suddenly opened a great mouth and

HOWLED!

And then another surprising thing happened! A second head poked up from under a covering of seaweed, and a voice shouted loudly, **'Tell your dog to keep off!** Mine will **fight him!** And **GO AWAY, ALL OF YOU!'**

CHAPTER EIGHT

The second head was still poking out of its strange **SEAWEED-Y** hiding place.

'Hey!' yelled Julian. 'We **won't** hurt you. If you want help, we'll give it to you. **Come on out,** and **tell us** what **you're doing!'**

'All right. But if you try to catch me, I'll set **my dog** on you!' yelled back a defiant voice. 'He's a cross-bred **Alsatian** and he could **eat** up **your dog** in **one gulp!'**

And then the **SEAWEED** pile was heaved **UP** and **down**, and out came a scraggy, **wet boy.** He pulled the **SEAWEED** off the dog. The great animal shook itself, and gave one more **miserable howl.**

The Five were almost too astonished to say a word. The boy looked half scared. George spoke first. 'What are you doing on my island?'

'My name's **Bobby Loman.** I live with my **Granpop** in Kirrin Village. My mum and dad are dead, and I'm on my own – except for **Chippy** the **monkey** here, and **Chummy,** my **Alsatian.** I've **run away. That's all.'**

'No,' said Anne gently. 'That isn't all. Tell us everything, Bobby.'

'Oh, well – it's not much,' said Bobby. 'Granpop **hates Chippy,** because **he steals things.** And **Chummy costs** a lot to keep – and – and – you see, he bit someone last week – and Granpop said he was to be **put to sleep.'** Bobby began to cry, and the Alsatian nestled close to him and licked his cheek. **'He loves me!** He's the only person who does.'

George put her arms round Timmy. **'I'm GLAD** you came to **my island,'** said George. 'You and Chippy and Chummy can live here as long as you like. We'll bring you food each day, we'll . . .'

'Hold on, George,' said Julian. 'Don't make promises we can't keep. Let's go back to Kirrin Cottage and tell your mum about this – she'll know what's best to do.'

'Oh – what fun to have another dog and a monkey, as well as Timmy,' said Anne. 'Bobby – how did you come to the island, if you **didn't** have **a boat?'**

'Oh – that was easy,' said Bobby. 'I've got one of those **blow-up beds.** Chippy and I sailed on it, with **a spade** for **an oar** – and Chummy swam alongside. It's buried in the sand, so that nobody would see it. But I **didn't have any food,** so . . .'

'So you crept into our outhouse last night and took a bag of **dog biscuits** for **Chummy,** and some **fruit** for **Chippy,**' said Julian. 'What about **yourself?**'

'Oh – I've been eating the **dog biscuits,**' said Bobby. 'I took some *chocolate* too. **I'm sorry** about the stealing. I was desperate, you know.'

'Come on – let's get back home,' said Julian, seeing that Bobby was tired out, cold, wet, and probably **very** hungry.'

Bobby looked doubtful, but said no more. He cuddled up to Timmy and Chummy, who both took turns at licking him. Chippy the monkey was very lively and leapt from one person to another, making a funny little chattering noise. He took Dick's handkerchief out of his pocket and pretended to blow his nose on it.

'Hey – you're **not** to take things from people, **I've told you that before!**' said Bobby. 'Ooooh – that reminds me – he brought this **shoe** to me this morning – does it belong to any of you?' And out of his pocket he took – **one red sandal!**

Anne gave a delighted yell. **'OH!** It's **mine.** I missed it this morning. Oh good – now I won't have to buy a new pair! Chippy – you really are a monkey!'

CHAPTER NINE

George's mother was very astonished to see a monkey, a dog and another boy added to the Five when they arrived at Kirrin Cottage.

'Who are all these?' she said. 'I don't mind the dog, George, but I will not have a monkey running loose in the house.'

'He can **sleep** in the **shed,** Mum,' said George. 'Mum, this is **Bobby** – he ran away from his grandfather.'

'Bobby? Bobby Loman do you mean?' said Mrs Kirrin. 'He was in the **papers today.**

Bobby, your grandfather is **very** unhappy and **worried.** I'm sure he would never have had your dog destroyed. He only said that in the **heat of the moment –** when he was **very cross!'**

Bobby looked rather scared at Mrs Kirrin's forthright words. George put her arm around his shoulder.

'Mum!' she said, 'I'm sure I'd run away if you threatened to do anything to Timmy – so I do understand why Bobby ran away to my island. Well – sailed away!'

Things were soon settled. Mrs Kirrin rang up the police to tell them **Bobby was safe.** Then she rang up his grandfather and told him the news too. The old man was **so relieved** that he could hardly thank Mrs Kirrin enough.

Bobby was
allowed to stay the night, and
slept in the kitchen on a sofa, with **Chippy**
cuddled **beside him,** and **Chummy on
his feet. Upstairs** George was in bed
with **Timmy on her feet,** talking about
the excitements of the day.

'How's your tooth?' asked Anne,
suddenly remembering the night before, when
George had had such bad toothache, and **seen
a light** on Kirrin Island.

74

'Tooth? **What tooth?**' said George, surprised. She had forgotten all about it. 'Oh, the one I had out. Doesn't it seem **AGES** since this morning!' She put her tongue into the space where the tooth had been. 'I think a new one's growing already. I wish I had teeth like Timmy – snowy white – strong – fierce. I'd like to be able to show all my teeth, when I feel **really angry!**'

Anne laughed. 'Well – you almost manage it now,' she said.

'Hey – what's
the matter with Timmy?
He's pretty restless tonight.
Look – he's gone to the door.
He wants to go out.'

    'All he wants is to go and have **a
talk to Chummy,'** said George. 'All right,
Tim. You can go down to the kitchen and sleep
with Chummy if you like.'

Timmy pattered down the stairs as soon as the bedroom door was opened. He scraped at the kitchen door and Bobby got up to open it. He was surprised and pleased to see Timmy, who licked him lavishly, and then went to lie beside the pleased Alsatian.

George took one more look out of the window before she got into bed – and gave a sudden exclamation.

'Anne – I think there's a light on Kirrin Island again. Anne – **come** and **look!**'

'Don't be an idiot,' said Anne, sleepily. 'You don't think we're going to start this adventure all over again, do you? It's FINISHED, George, not just beginning. **Come back to bed.**'

George jumped into bed. 'It was a light,' she said, after a moment or two. 'But only a **shooting star!** What a pity! I'd have liked another adventure – wouldn't you, Anne?'

But Anne was fast asleep, dreaming of monkeys, red sandals, seaweed, big dogs and orange peel.